USBORNE
LEARN TO PLAY
OPERA
TUNES

Caroline Hooper

Designed by Joanne Pedley

Illustrated by Ross Watton

Additional illustrations by David Cuzik

Edited by Emma Danes

Music arrangements by Caroline Hooper
Research assistant: Eileen O'Brien
Music consultant: Ruth Thackeray

Contents

What is opera?   3

How opera began   4
Euridice	Peri	6
Orfeo	Monteverdi	7
Armide	Lully	8
Ormindo	Cavalli	10
Dido and Aeneas	Purcell	11

Opera in the 18th century   12
Il Mitridate Eupatore	A. Scarlatti	14
The Beggar's Opera	Pepusch	15
Rinaldo	Handel	16
La Serva Padrona	Pergolesi	18
Castor et Pollux	Rameau	19
Orfeo ed Euridice	Gluck	20
The Marriage of Figaro	Mozart	21
The Magic Flute	Mozart	22

Opera in the 19th century   24
Fidelio	Beethoven	26
The Barber of Seville	Rossini	27
L'Elisir d'Amore	Donizetti	28
Nabucco	Verdi	29
Rigoletto	Verdi	30
Die Walküre	Wagner	31
Die Fledermaus	J. Strauss	32
Carmen	Bizet	33
La Bohème	Puccini	34
Turandot	Puccini	35

Opera in Eastern Europe   36
A Life for the Tsar	Glinka	38
The Bartered Bride	Smetana	39
Boris Godunov	Musorgsky	40
Eugene Onegin	Tchaikovsky	42
Prince Igor	Borodin	43

Opera stories   44
Playing the pieces   46
Index   48

About this book

The music in each section appears in the order in which it was written. Above each piece you can see the title of the tune in the original language and in English, as well as the name of the opera it comes from. After the name of the opera you can find out the date when it was first performed. On pages 44 and 45 you can read about the story of each opera, and on pages 46 and 47 there are some hints about how to play the pieces.

What is opera?

The cover for *Turandot* by the Italian composer Giacomo Puccini (1858-1924)

An opera is a type of play in which all or most of the words are sung. The singers wear costumes and there is often spectacular scenery on the stage. An orchestra usually accompanies the singers, as well as playing other music before the opera starts and between the songs.

The cover for *Carmen* by the French composer Georges Bizet (1838-1875)

Opera began in Italy, at the end of the 16th century. At first the words were all in Italian, but before long people started to write operas in other languages too. Over the years, many different types of opera have developed. Some of them are funny, others are serious. Often the stories are very complicated. Today, the words of an opera are often translated into the language of the country where it is being performed. This helps the audience to understand what is happening.

Dame Gwyneth Jones, a soprano from Wales, and Plácido Domingo, a Spanish tenor, in *Turandot* by Puccini

Opera voices

Different types of voices have special names in opera. The chart below shows you how high or low the most common voices are, starting with the highest, soprano.

Female	Male
soprano —	
mezzo-soprano —	
contralto —	countertenor
	tenor
	baritone
	bass

Shirley Verrett, a mezzo-soprano from America, in *Carmen* by Bizet

José Carreras, a Spanish tenor, in *Samson et Dalila* by the French composer Camille Saint-Saëns (1835-1921)

How opera began

Music has always played an important part in theatrical performances, but its role has changed gradually over the years. For centuries music has been added to plays to make them more interesting. Sometimes it was used to accompany singers and dancers on stage. At other times it was used to express the mood of a play, a little like some film and television music does today.

An 8th-century painting of a theatrical performance

Musicians accompanying an 18th-century play

Early musical plays

Although most historians say that opera began at the end of the 16th century, its origins can be traced much further back in history. In ancient Greek and Roman times, over 2,000 years ago, one of the most popular forms of entertainment was mime (acting without speaking). While the actors mimed on stage, musicians played to accompany them.

Fragments of Greek pottery showing a performance of a mime

A mystery play

Later, around the 10th century, religious plays set to music were often performed outside churches to attract worshipers. These performances became known as mystery plays.

In the 12th and 13th centuries, a type of play developed based on the songs of traveling musicians known as troubadours and minstrels.

A 13th-century musical play

The minstrels' plays were called pastoral plays because the songs described country life.

During the 15th century, another type of musical play called a *masque* became popular, especially in England. This was a combination of songs, dances and poetry, in which everyone wore costumes and masks to disguise themselves.

A masque in the 16th century

The first operas

At the end of the 16th century, a group of Italian poets and musicians called the *Camerata* began to experiment with new types of songwriting. They believed that most songs at that time were too complicated, and that the words were too difficult to hear. They tried to make their music simple and memorable, and the words clear and easy to understand.

At first they used these ideas for short songs, but they soon applied them to longer musical plays. Gradually these became known as operas (the word *opera* means "work" in Latin). The very first opera produced by the *Camerata* was *Dafne*, written in 1597 by Jacopo Peri (1561-1633), who was a composer, and Ottavio Rinuccini (1562-1621), a poet. As well as writing the music for the opera, Peri sang in the very first performances.

The stage of a 17th-century opera house

Dame Janet Baker, a mezzo-soprano from England, playing the part of Poppaea in a performance of *The Coronation of Poppaea* by Monteverdi

Early performances

At first, operas were performed in the homes of wealthy noblemen but, as they became more popular, special theaters were built for public performances. The first public opera house, Teatro San Cassiano, was opened in Venice in 1637. Several operas by the famous Italian composer Claudio Monteverdi (1567-1643) were first performed in public at this opera house.

Before long, opera began to spread throughout Europe. In France, short sections of opera were added to ballets (dances which tell a story). These entertainments became known as *opéra-ballets*. Later, some composers such as Jean-Baptiste Lully (1632-1687) began to write operas in a similar style to the Italian composers. In France, however, they were still usually performed in private houses.

A portrait of Lully

Writing operas down

Very few operas from the 17th century survive today. This is partly because composers often only wrote down two lines of music, the highest and the lowest. They organized the middle parts during rehearsals.

Manuscript of Monteverdi's *Orfeo* showing only the highest and lowest lines of music

Composers often changed songs to suit particular soloists, and adapted the music according to the number of singers and musicians available for each performance. This number often depended on the size of the opera house.

The American soprano Jessye Norman, playing the part of Dido in *Dido and Aeneas* by the English composer Henry Purcell (1659-1695)

Peri (1561-1633)

Nel puro ardor della più bella stella
The bright shining of the fairest star

from *Euridice* (1600)

Opera performers

During the 17th century, wealthy noblemen who put on operas in their own houses often took part in them as well. Even Louis XIV, the king of France, frequently performed in operas and ballets. Sometimes composers appeared in operas too. Peri, who composed some of the very first operas, was a famous singer and actor, and took part in many early opera performances.

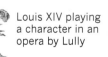

Louis XIV playing a character in an opera by Lully

Peri in costume for one of his own operas

Monteverdi (1567-1643)

Lasciate i monti, lasciate i fonti
Leave the hills, leave the fountains

from **Orfeo** (1607)

Stage machinery

In the 17th century, operas often contained spectacular special effects, such as clouds moving in the sky, or a ship sailing across an ocean. Complicated stage machinery was needed to do this. The picture on the right shows a design for some machinery to make a horse and carriage move across the stage. The machinery itself would have been hidden so the audience could not see it.

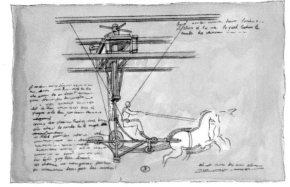

Lully (1632-1687)

Air de la gloire

Air to glory

from *Armide* (1686)

Cavalli (1602-1676)

Chi, chi, chi mi toglie al die?
Who, who, who will take me from the light?

from *Ormindo* (1644)

Purcell (1659-1695)

Sailor's chorus

from *Dido and Aeneas* (1689)

Allegro molto

Opera in the 18th century

During the 18th century, opera became more popular than ever. This was partly because, as more opera houses were built, many people began to use them as social meeting places. While the opera was being performed on stage, the audience, instead of sitting quietly, played cards and chatted to their friends, occasionally stopping to watch a well-known scene or aria.

Around this time composers began to write more and more of their music down. This meant that operas written at the end of the 18th century, unlike many earlier ones, hardly changed from one performance to another. Many have survived and are still performed today.

A scene from an *opera seria*

George Frideric Handel (1685-1759) wrote many operas in the *opera seria* style.

An *opera seria* was usually divided into two or three sections called "acts". To lighten the mood, comic scenes called *intermezzi* were sometimes performed between each act.

Intermezzi were usually acted out by two people, and were often inspired by real life situations. Gradually these comic scenes became so popular that composers began to write whole new operas in the style of *intermezzi*. In Italy, this new comic style of opera became known as *opera buffa*.

Opera buffa stories were about real people, not gods and goddesses.

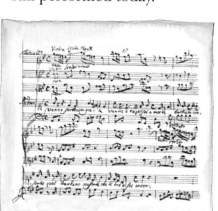

A manuscript for an 18th-century opera showing all the parts written out in detail

New types of opera

At first, operas were very serious. They were usually based on stories from ancient history and mythology. In these operas all the words were sung. The stories always had a happy ending in which the villain was caught and the hero was rewarded for his bravery. In Italy, this type of opera was known as *opera seria*, which means "serious opera".

A scene from *The Marriage of Figaro*, an *opera buffa* by Mozart

Similar types of comic opera were also developing in other countries. One of the earliest comic operas was written in England in 1728. This was *The Beggar's Opera*, by John Gay (1685-1732) and Johann Christoph Pepusch (1667-1752). The music was based on traditional tunes. It was the first opera in which the villains were seen as heroes. Unlike earlier operas, which were watched mainly by noblemen, this new type, called ballad opera, was very popular among ordinary people.

A scene from *The Beggar's Opera* by Pepusch

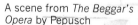

Later comic styles

In Germany, a translation of a ballad opera inspired a new opera style called *Singspiel*, which means "song-play". These operas were light-hearted and often included spoken words. *The Magic Flute* (1791) is a famous opera in this style by Wolfgang Amadeus Mozart (1756-1791).

In France the new comic style was known as *opéra comique*. At first it was used for sideshows at fairs, where the actors made fun of serious opera by singing the words of ordinary plays to made-up tunes.

A performance of an *opéra-comique* at a fair

Before long, *opéra comique* became just as popular as the serious opera it mocked.

Famous opera singers

The New Zealand soprano Dame Kiri Te Kanawa, playing Donna Elvira in a production of Mozart's opera *Don Giovanni*

Yvonne Kenny, a soprano from Australia, in a performance of *Alcina* by Handel

Bryn Terfel, a Welsh baritone and Sylvia McNair, a soprano from America, in *The Marriage of Figaro* by Mozart

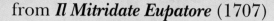

A. Scarlatti (1660-1725)

Se il trono domando al Cielo
If I ask heaven to grant me the throne

from *Il Mitridate Eupatore* (1707)

The libretto

Some opera stories are very complicated. When opera began, each person in the audience was given a booklet containing all the words of the songs to help them understand the story. If the words were in a foreign language, there was usually a translation as well. This booklet was called the libretto (in Italian the word *libretto* means "little book").

Carlo Goldoni wrote librettos for comic operas.

Lorenzo da Ponte wrote the librettos for three operas by Mozart.

Pepusch (1667-1752)

Polly you must have toyed and kissed

from *The Beggar's Opera* (1728)

Larghetto

During the 18th century, the whole theater was lit, making it easy for people to read the libretto during a performance. Later, only the stage was lit, so theaters began to sell brief outlines of the story for people to read before the opera began. These were called programs. If you go to an opera today, it is a good idea to read the program before the performance begins.

Pietro Metastasio wrote over 70 librettos.

John Gay wrote the libretto for *The Beggar's Opera*.

Handel (1685-1759)

Lascia ch'io pianga
Leave me in sorrow

from **Rinaldo** (1711)

Aria and recitative

As opera started to become more popular, some singers, such as the ones shown on the right, became very famous. Good singers could attract large audiences and help new operas to become successful, so composers began to write special songs to allow them to show off their talents. These songs were called arias. Many of the most popular opera tunes today are arias.

Carlo Scalzi   Senesino   Irena Tomeoni

Rameau (1683-1764)

Que tout gemise, que tout s'unise
Let all lament, let all unite

from *Castor et Pollux* (1737)

Hanswurst
Anton Raaff
Farinelli

The music in arias was often so decorative that it was difficult for the audience to understand the words. Because of this, arias were normally linked by simpler songs that explained what was going on in the story. The rhythm of these songs usually followed the pattern of speech very closely, so the words were easier to understand. This type of music was known as recitative.

Gluck (1714-1787)

Che farò senza Euridice?
What shall I do without Euridice?

from **Orfeo ed Euridice** (1762)

Mozart (1756-1791)

Voi, che sapete che cosa è amor
You who know what love is

from *The Marriage of Figaro* (1786)

Mozart (1756-1791)

Bei Männern, welche Liebe fühlen

Men who feel love's emotion

from ***The Magic Flute*** (1791)

Behind the scenes of an opera

The picture on the right shows some backstage preparations for a performance of *The Magic Flute*. There is always a lot to do before an opera begins. The singers have to arrange their hair, put on stage makeup and dress up in their costumes. They also have to make sure all of their props (objects needed during the opera) are in the right places, so they are ready to take on stage.

Shortly before the opera starts, the singers have to warm up their voices. They do this by singing a series of notes, gradually getting higher or lower. It is important for them to do this before a performance so they relax all the muscles around their throats. This helps them to sing very loudly and clearly so that the audience can hear all the words.

Opera in the 19th century

Charles Edward Horn, a famous 19th-century opera singer

Throughout most of the 18th century, people believed that thought and reason were the basis of art, music and literature. But around the end of the century, many writers, painters and composers began to say that art should be inspired more by feelings and emotions. They were part of a trend that is now known as Romanticism.

Jenny Lind, one of the most famous sopranos of the 19th century

The French Revolution

During the late 18th century, ordinary people in France began to rebel against the extravagant lifestyles of the royal family and other wealthy noblemen. They wanted their own poor living conditions to be improved. The fighting that resulted became known as the French Revolution.

A scene from *Fidelio* by Beethoven

One of the most famous operas inspired by the Revolution is *Fidelio*, by the German composer Ludwig van Beethoven (1770-1827).

French rebels attacking a prison

The Revolution had a strong effect on opera during the early part of the 19th century. At first, ordinary people condemned opera as an entertainment for rich people. But it was not long before composers began to use the political unrest as a theme for their operas. Soon opera was seen as a means of promoting the cause of the ordinary people. It became more popular than ever, not only in France, but throughout Western Europe.

Grand opera

A new type of opera began to develop in Western Europe around 1830. It was known as grand opera because it involved spectacular costumes and scenery, and often incorporated huge crowd scenes. The stories were sometimes based on legends, but many were about relationships between people of different religions and backgrounds. The German composer Richard Wagner (1813-1883) wrote many grand operas.

A scene from *Rienzi* by Wagner

Operetta

During the 17th and 18th centuries, the word operetta was used to describe a short opera. By the middle of the 19th century, it became the name for a new style of opera which developed from French 18th-century *opéra comique*. These new operettas were usually light-hearted,

The cover of *Die Fledermaus* by Strauss

with some spoken words as well as the songs. Often they also included dances. One of the most famous 19th-century operettas is *Die Fledermaus* by an Austrian composer called Johann Strauss (1825-1899).

Claques

In the 19th century, there were groups of people who called themselves *claques*. They were employed by singers and people who had invested money in an opera, to go to performances and clap loudly. (The word *claque* comes from the French verb meaning "to clap".) People paid *claques* to help make an opera popular and successful. Sometimes they also paid them to make sure an opera failed, by booing and shouting at the singers on stage.

Members of a *claque* among an audience

Claques used to spread out among the audience and wait for a signal from their leader, who would be carefully positioned so that the others could see him. They also tried to influence other members of the audience, by talking to them before, and during, the performance. Often *claques* were paid according to how loudly they clapped or booed.

Famous opera singers

Benjamin Luxon, an English baritone, in a performance of *Falstaff* by the Italian composer Giuseppe Verdi (1813-1901)

Luciano Pavarotti, an Italian tenor, playing the part of Nemorino in a performance of *L'Elisir d'Amore* by the Italian composer Gaetano Donizetti (1797-1848)

Dame Joan Sutherland, a soprano from Australia, in a performance of *Lucrezia Borgia* by Donizetti

Beethoven (1770-1827)

Mir ist so wunderbar
I feel wonderful

from *Fidelio* (1805)

Andante sostenuto

Overtures

An overture is a piece of music played before an opera begins. Originally it announced the start of a performance and allowed the audience time to settle down. It was usually lively and exciting, but was not linked to the music that followed. Later, some composers began to use the overture to introduce themes from the opera. Today, opera overtures are often played at the beginning of orchestral concerts.

This is an early title page for *The Barber of Seville* by Rossini. The overture for this is often played at the beginning of orchestral concerts.

Rossini (1792-1868)

Overture

from *The Barber of Seville* (1816)

Allegro vivace

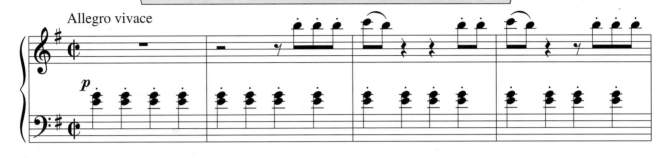

Donizetti (1797-1848)

Una furtiva lagrima
A furtive tear

from *L'Elisir d'Amore* (1832)

Larghetto

The first recordings

Some of the first recordings ever made were of opera singers. Recordings allowed opera to spread to a wider audience, and made the singers even more well-known. On the right you can see two early recording stars.

Enrico Caruso, an Italian tenor

Dame Nellie Melba, an Australian soprano

— 28 —

Verdi (1813-1901)

Coro di schiavi ebrei
Chorus of the Hebrew slaves

from *Nabucco* (1841)

Verdi (1813-1901)

La donna è mobile
Women are frivolous

from **Rigoletto** (1851)

Wagner (1813-1883)

Ritt der Walküren
Ride of the Valkyries

from *Die Walküre* (1856)

J. Strauss (1825-1899)

Du und du
You and you

from *Die Fledermaus* (1874)

Tempo di valse

Costumes

Costumes are very important in helping to set the scene of an opera. They enable the audience to identify the characters and to guess a little bit about them. For example, a wealthy character might wear a very elaborate costume. An evil character might wear dark clothes and heavy makeup. On the right you can see some costume designs for 19th-century operas.

A very rich character in *L'Elisir d'Amore* by Donizetti

A warrior in *Die Walküre* by Wagner

Bizet (1838-1875)

Toréador, en garde!
Toreador, fight well!

from *Carmen* (1875)

Alla marcia

A costume for a beautiful princess in *Turandot* by Puccini

A comic character in *Rigoletto* by Verdi

A costume for a poor woman in *Fidelio* by Beethoven

An evil character in *Turandot* by Puccini

Puccini (1858-1924)

O Mimì, tu più non torni!

Ah Mimì, you will never come back!

from *La Bohème* (1896)

Puccini (1858-1924)

Nessun dorma
None shall sleep

from *Turandot* (1926)

Opera in Eastern Europe

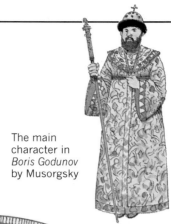

The main character in *Prince Igor* by Borodin

The main character in *Boris Godunov* by Musorgsky

Opera first spread to Eastern Europe in the early part of the 18th century, but it was not until the 19th century that it really began to flourish. Composers at this time were strongly influenced by the traditional music from their own countries. Their operas were often based on folk tales or national history.

Until the early 19th century, music in Eastern Europe was dominated by Western European styles. But, around this time, many people were becoming interested in the customs and traditions of their countries. Composers in many parts of Europe began to write music based on folk songs and dances.

A scene from *A Life for the Tsar* by Glinka

Russian folk dancers and musicians

The first operas to be performed in Eastern Europe were from Italy. As they gradually became popular, composers in Russia began to write their own operas. At first they made them similar to the Italian operas, but before long they started to develop their own distinctive style.

The first of these new distinctive operas was *A Life for the Tsar* by the Russian composer Mikhail Ivanovich Glinka (1804-1857).

The "mighty handful"

Around the middle of the 19th century, a group of five Russian composers decided to concentrate on writing music which sounded unmistakably Russian. They became known as the "mighty handful". Two of the most famous operas by members of this group were *Boris Godunov*, by Modest Musorgsky (1839-1881) and *Prince Igor*, by Alexander Borodin (1833-1887).

Pyotr Il'yich Tchaikovsky (1840-1893), another Russian composer, was impressed by the music of the "mighty handful", and decided to try

making his own music sound more Russian. Previously he had been successfully writing music in a Western European style. When he combined this style with Russian folk tunes, his music became more popular than ever.

The Bolshoi Theater in Moscow, famous for opera and ballet performances

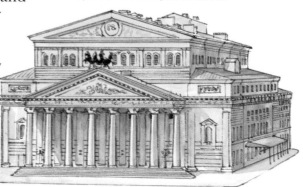

Opera in Bohemia

In Bohemia, now part of the Czech Republic, the influence of Western Europe was so great in the early 19th century that in schools children were not taught their own language and traditions. Around the middle of the century, the people started to rebel. They wanted to revive the Czech language, and traditional styles of Bohemian music and theater.

Bedřich Smetana

About the same time, Bedřich Smetana (1824-1884), a Czech composer, returned home to Bohemia after living in Western Europe. He began to learn to speak Czech, and started to write music based on Czech folk tunes and legends. One of his most famous operas is *The Bartered Bride.*

Original manuscript of *The Bartered Bride* by Smetana

Famous opera singers

Sergei Leiferkus, a Russian baritone, and Anna Tomowa-Sintow, a Bulgarian soprano, in a performance of *Prince Igor* by Borodin

Willard White, a Jamaican bass, in a performance of *Khovanshchina* by Musorgsky

Glinka (1804-1857)

Vstuplénie v déistvie trét'e
Introduction to Act Three

from *A Life for the Tsar* (1762)

Smetana (1824-1884)

Pojd' sem, holka, toc se, holka
Come on girls, let's be merry

from *The Bartered Bride* (1866)

Moderato

Musorgsky (1839-1881)

Sláva tebyé
Glory to thee our God

from *Boris Godunov* (1874)

Scenery

Opera performances often require lots of scenery. Depending on the story, the setting might change from a bleak prison cell in one scene, to an entire city in another. All the scenery has to be carefully designed and constructed so that it looks as interesting as possible to the audience, but can be moved around easily during a performance. Russian operas are particularly famous for the huge amounts of magnificent scenery they often use.

The scenery for a performance of *Boris Godunov* by Musorgsky

Tchaikovsky (1840-1893)

Dévitsy krasávitsy
Dear companions

from **Eugene Onegin** (1887)

Borodin (1833-1887)

Chor' poloveckich' devusek'
Chorus of the Polovtsian maidens

from *Prince Igor* (1890)

On these two pages you can read about the stories of the operas in this book. The name the opera is most commonly known by is given first, followed by the original name or an English translation (where the title is not the name of a character).

Euridice

Orfeo goes to the underworld to rescue the woman he loves, Euridice. The king of the underworld agrees to release her as long as Orfeo does not look at her until they reach Earth. At the last minute Orfeo turns around and Euridice is lost. They are reunited in heaven by Orfeo's father, Apollo.

Orfeo

This is based on the same story as *Euridice*.

Armide

Renaud is captured by Armide, a sorceress, who takes him to her enchanted palace in the desert. He is rescued by his friends, Ubalde and a Danish knight. Armide flies into a rage and orders demons to destroy her palace.

Ormindo

Ormindo is in love with Erisbe, wife of Ariadeno. They prepare to run away, but are captured by Ariadeno, who orders them to be poisoned. The poison is only a sleeping potion, however, and on discovering that Ormindo is his long-lost son, Ariadeno renounces his claim on Erisbe.

Dido and Aeneas

The love affair of Dido, Queen of Carthage, and Aeneas, a Trojan prince, is doomed by an evil sorceress who tricks Aeneas into leaving Carthage with his Trojan fleet. Dido is heartbroken and dies.

Il Mitridate Eupatore

Mitridate and Issicratea decide to overthrow Farnace, who has seized the throne of Pontus. Disguised as Egyptians, they trick Farnace into believing that he will receive the head of Mitridate in a casket. As Farnace awaits his trophy, Mitridate kills him. Mitridate is then crowned King of Pontus.

The Beggar's Opera

Peachum and his wife are very angry when they discover that their daughter, Polly, has secretly married Captain Macheath, a notorious highwayman. Macheath, thrown into prison by Peachum, promises to marry Lucy Lockit when she helps him to escape. Following a squabble between Polly and Lucy, Macheath is recaptured and sentenced to be hanged. The opera ends happily, though, when Macheath is set free.

Rinaldo

Goffredo, an army captain, has promised Rinaldo, a brave soldier, his daughter Almirena's hand in marriage if the city of Jerusalem is captured. At the request of Argante, King of Jerusalem, Almirena is captured by the sorceress Armida and held prisoner in her enchanted palace. Rinaldo destroys Armida's palace with the help of a magician, and is reunited with Almirena.

La Serva Padrona (The Maid as Mistress)

When Uberto decides to find a wife, Serpina, his servant, insists that he marries her. Uberto refuses, so Serpina tries to make him jealous by pretending Vespone, a servant in disguise, is her fiancé. Her plan succeeds and Uberto eventually marries her.

Castor et Pollux

When Castor is killed, Telaira, the woman he loved, is overcome with grief. She persuades Pollux, his twin, to ask his father, Jupiter, to restore Castor to life. Jupiter agrees, but only if Pollux takes Castor's place in the underworld. When Castor realizes this, he agrees to swap places for one day only. When he returns to the underworld, Jupiter makes him immortal, and the twins are reunited.

Orfeo ed Euridice

This story is the same as *Euridice*, but at the end, Euridice is restored to life by Cupid.

The Marriage of Figaro (Le Nozze di Figaro)

Susanna, maid to Countess Almaviva, is engaged to Figaro, Count Almaviva's valet, but the Count has also professed his love for her. To punish the Count for being unfaithful to the Countess, the women play a trick on him. He soon begs forgiveness.

The Magic Flute (Die Zauberflöte)

Tamino is in love with Pamina, daughter of the wicked Queen of the Night. When the Queen tells him Pamina has been captured by a wicked sorcerer called Sarastro, Tamino goes to rescue her, with the help of his magic flute and Papageno, the birdcatcher. Sarastro turns out to be a wise and noble man and, after many trials, Tamino and Pamina are reunited, and the Queen is driven away.

Fidelio

Pizarro, governor of a gloomy fortress, has wrongfully imprisoned his enemy Florestan, a

Spanish nobleman. Leonora, Florestan's wife, disguises herself as a man called Fidelio. She becomes assistant to Rocco, the chief jailer, and saves her husband's life.

The Barber of Seville (Il Barbiere di Siviglia)

The barber Figaro, a popular busybody, helps Count Almaviva to outwit old Dr. Bartolo and marry Rosina, Bartolo's ward.

L'Elisir d'Amore (The Elixir of Love)

The rich and beautiful Adina laughs at the peasant Nemorino who loves her. In desperation, Nemorino takes a love potion which enables him to win her.

Nabucco

When King Nabucco captures Jerusalem, he leaves his daughter Fenena to rule Babylon in his place. Abigaille, believed to be the King's eldest daughter, but who is really a slave, becomes jealous and throws the King into prison. As she is about to execute Fenena, the King escapes and stops her.

Rigoletto

The Duke of Mantua has fallen in love with Gilda, daughter of his jester, Rigoletto. Rigoletto, who has made many enemies with his cruel jokes, is tricked by courtiers into abducting Gilda. Seeking revenge, Rigoletto plots to murder the Duke, but his plan goes horribly wrong when Gilda is killed instead.

Die Walküre (The Valkyrie)

Siegmund seeks refuge in a house in the forest. Here he meets Sieglinde, wife of his evil enemy, Hunding. They fall in love and run away together, unaware that they are brother and sister. Fricka, the goddess of marriage, is outraged and orders her husband Wotan to punish them. Wotan tells Brünnhilde, a Valkyrie (warrior), to kill Siegmund. Brünnhilde disobeys, but Wotan interferes and Siegmund dies. Brünnhilde manages to save Sieglinde, but she is severely punished by Wotan.

Die Fledermaus (The Bat)

Eisenstein should be spending eight days in prison for insulting a policeman, but is persuaded by a friend, Dr. Falke, to go to a costume ball. There Eisenstein meets his own wife, who is also in disguise, and falls in love with her.

Carmen

Don José, a corporal, has fallen in love with Carmen, a girl who sells cigarettes. They run away to the mountains with a band of smugglers and gypsies, but Carmen soon grows tired of José and turns her attention to Escamillo, a bullfighter. Insanely jealous, José kills Carmen.

La Bohème (The Bohemians)

This story tells of a group of poor artists and writers in Paris, and the tragic love affair between Rodolfo and Mimì. Mimì has a fatal illness and dies.

Turandot

Calaf has fallen in love with the cruel Princess Turandot, who kills all who love her if they fail to pass her test. Calaf passes the test, but Turandot is reluctant to marry him. Calaf agrees to give her up if she can discover his true identity. Turandot fails, but falls in love with Calaf, who finally reveals he is a prince and marries her.

A Life for the Tsar (Zhizn za Tsar)

This opera tells the story of Ivan Susanin, who gave up his life to prevent the Russian Tsar from being captured by Polish soldiers.

The Bartered Bride (Prodaná nevesta)

Jenik is the long-lost son of Micha, but he has kept his identity a secret. Mařenka is in love with Jenik, and is heartbroken when she hears that he has been bribed by Kečal, the matchmaker, to give her up to the son of Micha. She only knows of one son of Micha and has no wish to marry him. She is overjoyed when Jenik reveals his true identity.

Boris Godunov

Having arranged the murder of Dimitri, heir to the throne of Russia, Boris is crowned Tsar. He soon hears rumors that Dimitri is still alive and has returned to claim his inheritance, though it is actually a man called Grigory pretending to be Dimitri. Boris is overcome with fear and guilt, and dies as Grigory and his troops arrive in Moscow.

Eugene Onegin

Tatiana falls in love with Eugene Onegin, but he tells her that he does not want to marry anyone. After killing his friend Lenski in a duel, Onegin spends many years in the wilderness. When he returns he falls in love with Tatiana, but it is too late as she is already married.

Prince Igor (Knjaz' Igor)

Prince Igor and his son, Vladimir, have been captured by enemy troops. Igor eventually escapes, but Vladimir is in love with the daughter of the enemy leader and remains behind.

Playing the pieces

In this section, you can find some hints on playing the pieces in this book. When you are learning a piece, it is often better to practice each hand separately, slowly at first, until you can play the notes comfortably. Then try them separately at the correct speed, and finally try playing both hands together. There are suggestions for fingerings in the music, but if these do not feel comfortable, try to figure out your own. If you want to begin with the simplest pieces in the book, try *The Beggar's Opera* on page 15 and *La Serva Padrona* on page 18.

Euridice (page 6)

Be careful in measures 7 and 17, as you may find the fingering a little bit hard at first. Make sure you keep a steady beat in these measures. *Allegretto* means "fairly fast".

Orfeo (page 7)

Before trying the whole piece, practice measures 1 to 8 until you can play them without any mistakes. Then try measures 9 to 16, learning the fingerings very carefully in each hand before putting both hands together. Practice these measures slowly at first, until you are sure of the notes. Then try playing them at the correct speed.

Armide (page 8)

Play the grace notes in measures 7, 34 and 38 very quickly, just before the main beat. The clef changes several times in the left-hand part, so always make sure you know which clef you are playing in. On the second beat of measure 7, play the G in the left-hand part with your third finger, then quickly switch to your thumb. *Moderato* means "at a moderate speed".

Ormindo (page 10)

The sign before the chords in the right-hand part of measures 1, 2 and 12 tells you to play these notes like a very quick arpeggio, but keeping your fingers down once you have pressed each key. You may find it a little difficult to keep a steady beat as you go from measure 15 to measure 16. Practice these two measures on their own until you can play them smoothly. *Largo* means "slow and broad", *dolce* means "sweet and gentle" and *espressivo* means "expressive".

Dido and Aeneas (page 11)

The rhythm is a little difficult in measures 21, 22, 25 and 26 , so practice these measures on their own at first. In measures 25 and 26, make sure you play the right-hand and left-hand parts at exactly the same time. *Allegro molto* means "very fast", but it is a good idea to practice the piece slowly at first.

Il Mitridate Eupatore (page 14)

Play the left-hand part fairly quietly to stop it from sounding too heavy. In measures 15 to 18 you have to play triplets with your right hand and eighth notes with your left hand. You can practice this rhythm by saying the words "fried eggs and ham". Tap your right hand to the words "fried", "eggs" and "ham", and your left hand to the words "fried" and "and".

The Beggar's Opera (page 15)

Try to play this very smoothly, without leaving any gaps between the left-hand chords. Keep a steady beat throughout the piece. *Larghetto* means "slow, but not as slow as *largo*". You may already know this tune as *Golden Slumbers*.

Rinaldo (page 16)

The fingering for this piece is fairly hard, so practice both hands separately until you can play it at a comfortable speed. There are some big leaps in the left-hand part, between measures 6 to 7, 20 to 21 and 40 to 41. Practice these pairs of measures until you can play them smoothly at the correct speed. Watch out for the accidentals, especially in measures 27 and 33.

La Serva Padrona (page 18)

Pay particular attention to the accented and staccato notes. Play the left-hand part very smoothly throughout the piece.

Castor et Pollux (page 19)

This is a funeral march, so play it very slowly and steadily. Watch out for the big leap in measure 6 in both hands. Practice this measure, moving from one chord to the other several times, before trying the whole piece. Try to make a big difference between the loud and quiet sections. *Lento* means "slow".

Orfeo ed Euridice (page 20)

Andante means "at a walking pace". Keep the left-hand part flowing, so it does not slow down. Play it fairly quietly so you can hear the tune. *D. C. al Fine* means "go back to the beginning and play until you reach the word *Fine*".

The Marriage of Figaro (page 21)

Play the left-hand part very gently and quietly. Measure 7 is fairly hard, so practice this on its own at first.

The Magic Flute (page 22)

You can practice this piece in two sections. The second section begins in measure 14. Practice the first section until you can play it comfortably without any mistakes. Measures 26 and 27 may need a little extra work, so practice these two measures on their own before trying the second section.

Fidelio (page 26)

Play the left-hand part very quietly, so that it doesn't drown out the tune in the right hand. The word *sostenuto* means "sustained", so try not to leave any gaps between the eighth note chords in the left hand.

The Barber of Seville (page 27)

Play this piece very lightly. The left-hand chords should be quieter than the right-hand notes. Try to make a big difference between the staccato and slurred notes in the right-hand part. Don't confuse the tenuto mark on the last note of measure 10 with the accents in the last measure. The tenuto mark tells you to hold the note for a little longer than usual, whereas the accent tells you to play the note more forcefully than usual. *Vivace* means "lively".

L'Elisir d'Amore (page 28)

Keep the left-hand part very smooth and even, and try not to rush the eighth notes. Play the grace notes in measures 9 and 12 just before the main beat.

Nabucco (page 29)

Keep the triplets in the left-hand part very even throughout the piece. Measures 7, 11 and 15 are fairly hard, so you might want to practice these measures on their own at first. Where you are playing a dotted eighth note and a sixteenth note with your right hand and a triplet with your left hand, the sixteenth note should come after the last note of the triplet. Watch out for the accidentals in measure 11. *Cantabile* means "in a singing style".

Rigoletto (page 30)

Play the staccato chords in the left-hand part very lightly. Make sure you play the accented notes a little stronger than the others.

Die Walküre (page 31)

D. S. al coda tells you to go back to the sign in measure 1, play until you reach the coda sign at the end of measure 7, then go to the measure marked coda (measure 17).

Die Fledermaus (page 32)

Watch out for the accidentals and keep the left-hand part very even. Make sure the three-note chords are not too heavy. *Tempo di valse* means "in the style of a waltz".

Carmen (page 33)

In measures 2 and 6, play the grace notes very quickly just before the main beat. The staccato chords in the left hand should sound very light. *Alla marcia* means "in the style of a march".

La Bohème (page 34)

Con ped. tells you to use the right-hand pedal. Hold the pedal down for the full length of each bass note, but always remember to release it just before the next bass note. There are some big leaps in the left hand, so practice this part on its own until you can play it without any mistakes. *Poco rit.* means "slowing down a little", and *a tempo* means "return to the original speed".

Turandot (page 35)

The fingering is fairly hard, so it is a good idea to practice each hand separately. When you can play each one at a comfortable speed, without any mistakes, then put them together. Watch out for the clef change in measure 18 in the left-hand part. Play the chord in measure 24 as a very quick arpeggio, but holding each note to the end of the chord. Pay particular attention to the dynamics in this piece.

A Life for the Tsar (page 38)

Watch out for the accidentals in this piece. You may need to practice measure 7 on its own at first. *Adagio* means "slow and leisurely".

The Bartered Bride (page 39)

Pay particular attention to the staccato and accented notes, as these give the piece its character. Play the grace notes as quickly as possible.

Boris Godunov (page 40)

Where you are playing eighth notes with both hands, make sure you play them at exactly the same time. Remember to play fairly quietly throughout the piece.

Eugene Onegin (page 42)

Some of the chords in the left-hand part are fairly hard. Practice them until you can play them smoothly, keeping a steady beat.

Prince Igor (page 43)

Play this fairly slowly, making sure the triplets are even. Play the chords in measures 9 to 12 as very quick arpeggios, but holding each note to the end of the chord. Try to keep the quarter note beat in the left-hand part very steady throughout the piece. *Con moto* means "with movement".

Index

Alcina, 13
A Life for the Tsar, 36, 38, 45, 47
aria, 18, 19
Armide, 8, 44, 46
audiences, 12, 25, 26, 28, 32

backstage, 22
Baker, Dame Janet, 5
ballad opera, 12, 13
ballet, 5
Beethoven, Ludwig van, 24, 26, 33
Bizet, Georges, 3, 33
Bohemia, 37
Bolshoi Theatre, 36
Boris Godunov, 36, 40, 45, 47
Borodin, Alexander, 36, 37, 43

Camerata, the, 4
Carmen, 3, 33, 45, 47
Carreras, José, 3
Caruso, Enrico, 28
Castor et Pollux, 19, 44, 46
Cavalli, Pietro Francesco, 10
claques, 25
comic opera, 12, 13, 14, 24
costumes, 3, 4, 23, 24, 32-33
Czech Republic, 37

Dafne, 4
dances, 4, 24, 36
Da Ponte, Lorenzo, 14
Dido and Aeneas, 5, 11, 44, 46
Die Fledermaus, 24, 32, 45, 47
Die Walküre, 31, 32, 45, 47
Domingo, Plácido, 3
Don Giovanni, 13
Donizetti, Gaetano, 25, 28, 32

Eugene Onegin, 42, 45, 47
Euridice, 6, 44, 46

Falstaff, 25
Fidelio, 24, 26, 33, 44, 47
folk songs, 36, 37
France, 5, 6, 13, 24
French Revolution, 24

Gay, John, 12, 15
Germany, 13
Glinka, Mikhail Ivanovich, 36, 38
Goldoni, Carlo, 14
Gluck, Christoph Willibald, 20
grand opera, 24
Greece (ancient), 4

Handel, George Frideric, 12, 13, 16
Horn, Charles Edward, 24

Il Mitridate Eupatore, 14, 44, 46
intermezzi, 12
Italy, 3, 4, 12, 36

Jones, Dame Gwyneth, 3

Kenny, Yvonne, 13
Khovanshchina, 37

La Bohème, 34, 45, 47
La Serva Padrona, 18, 44, 46
L'Elisir d'Amore, 25, 28, 32, 45, 47
Leiferkus, Sergei, 37
libretto, 14, 15
Lind, Jenny, 24
Louis XIV, 6
Lucrezia Borgia, 25
Lully, Jean-Baptiste, 5, 6, 8
Luxon, Benjamin, 25

manuscripts, 5, 12, 37
masks, 4
masque, 4
McNair, Sylvia, 13
Melba, Dame Nellie, 28
Metastasio, Pietro, 15
"mighty handful", the, 36
mime, 4
Monteverdi, Claudio, 5, 7
Mozart, Wolfgang Amadeus, 12, 13, 14, 21, 22
musical plays, 4
Musorgsky, Modest, 36, 37, 40
mystery plays, 4

Nabucco, 29, 45, 47
Norman, Jessye, 5

Orfeo ed Euridice, 44
opéra-ballets, 5
opera buffa, 12
opéra comique, 13, 24
opera houses, 5, 12
opera seria, 12
opera stories, 3, 12, 40, 44-5
opera voices, 3
operetta, 24
Orfeo, 7, 44, 46
Orfeo ed Euridice, 20, 46
Ormindo, 10, 44, 46
overtures, 26

pastoral plays, 4
Pavarotti, Luciano, 25
Pepusch, Johann Christoph, 12, 15
Pergolesi, Giovanni, 18
Peri, Jacopo, 4, 6
Prince Igor, 36, 37, 43, 45, 47
programs, 15
props, 22
Puccini, Giacomo, 3, 33, 34, 35
Purcell, Henry, 5, 11

Rameau, Jean-Philippe, 19
recitative, 18, 19
recordings, 28
rhythm, 19
Rienzi, 24
Rigoletto, 30, 33, 45, 47
Rinaldo, 16, 44, 46
Rinuccini, Ottavio, 4
Romanticism, 24
Rome (ancient), 4
Rossini, Gioachino, 26, 27
Russia, 36

Saint-Saëns, Camille, 3
Samson et Dalila, 3
Scarlatti, Alessandro, 14
scenery, 40
singers, 22, 23
Singspiel, 13
Smetana, Bedřich, 37, 39
stage machinery, 7
Strauss, Johann, 32
Sutherland, Dame Joan, 25

Tchaikovsky, Pyotr Il'yich, 36, 42
Te Kanawa, Dame Kiri, 13
Teatro San Cassiano , 5
Terfel, Bryn, 13
The Barber of Seville, 26, 27, 45, 47
The Bartered Bride, 37, 39, 45
The Beggar's Opera, 12, 15, 44, 46
The Coronation of Poppaea, 5
The Magic Flute, 13, 22, 44, 46
The Marriage of Figaro, 12, 21, 44, 46
Tomowa-Sintow, Anna, 37
Turandot, 3, 33, 35, 45, 47

Verdi, Guiseppe, 25, 29, 30, 33
Verrett, Shirley, 3

Wagner, Richard, 24, 31
warming up, 23
White, Willard, 37

Acknowledgements

The publishers would like to thank the following for the use of photographic material:
Donald Cooper/Photostage (page 3, top and bottom right; page 13, bottom; page 25, top, middle and bottom; page 37, bottom)
Zoë Dominic (page 3, bottom left; page 5, top and bottom)
Zoë Dominic/Richard H. Smith (page 13, top)
Catherine Ashmore (page 37, top)
Clive Barda/Performing Arts Library (page 13, middle)